Wee Willie Winkie

and Other Best-loved Rhymes

Wee Willie Winkie

and Other Best-loved Rhymes

Capella

This edition published in 2008 by Arcturus Publishing Limited
26/27 Bickels Yard, 151–153 Bermondsey Street,
London SE1 3HA

ISBN: 978-1-84837-137-8

Printed in China

Illustration by Ulkutay & Co Ltd
Compiler: Paige Weber

CONTENTS

Wee Willie Winkie

Wee Willie Winkie runs through the town,
Upstairs and downstairs in his nightgown,
Rapping at the windows, crying through each lock,
"Are the children in their beds? It's now eight o'clock!"

Little Bo Peep

Little Bo Peep has lost her sheep,
And can't tell where to find them.
Leave them alone, and they'll come home,
Wagging their tails behind them.

Little Bo Peep fell fast asleep,
And dreamed she heard them bleating.
But when she awoke she found it a joke,
For they were still all fleeting.

Then up she took her little crook,
Determined for to find them.
She found them indeed, but it made her heart bleed,
For they'd left their tails behind them.

It happened one day, as Bo Peep did stray
Over a meadow hard by,
That there she espied their tails, side by side,
All hung on a tree to dry.

She heaved a sigh and wiped her eye,
Then over the hills she raced,
And tried what she could, as a shepherdess should,
So each tail would be properly placed.

There Was an Old Woman Who Lived In a Shoe

There was an old woman
Who lived in a shoe.
She had so many children
She didn't know what to do.
She gave them some broth,
Without any bread,
Then kissed them all quickly
And sent them to bed.

Red Sky at Morning

Red sky at morning,
Sailors take warning.
Red sky at night,
Sailor's delight.

I Saw A Ship A-Sailing

I saw a ship a-sailing,
A-sailing on the sea.
And, oh, it was all laden,
With pretty things for thee!

There were comfits in the cabin,
And apples in the hold.
The sails were made of silk,
And the masts were made of gold.

The four and twenty sailors,
That stood between the decks,
Were four and twenty mice,
With gold chains about their necks.

The captain was a duck,
With a packet on his back.
And when the ship began to move,
The captain said, "Quack! Quack!"

The Little Robin

The little robin grieves
When the snow is on the ground,
For the trees have no leaves,
And no berries can be found.

The air is cold, the worms are hid.
For robin here, what can be done?
Let's throw around some crumbs of bread,
And then he'll live till snow is gone.

Simple Simon

Simple Simon met a pieman
Going to the fair.
Simple Simon asked the pieman,
"Let me taste your ware."

Said the pieman to Simple Simon,
"Show me first your penny."
Simple Simon told the pieman,
"Indeed I have not any."

Simple Simon went out fishing
For to catch a whale.
All the water he had got
Was in his mother's pail!

Simple Simon went to see
If plums grew on a thistle.
He pricked his finger very much,
Which made poor Simon whistle.

He went to catch a dickey bird,
And thought he could not fail,
Because he'd found a little salt
To put upon its tail.

He went for water with a sieve,
But soon it all ran through.
And now poor Simple Simon
Bids you a fond adieu.

Hickory, Dickory, Dock!

Hickory, dickory, dock!
The mouse ran up the clock.
The clock struck one,
The mouse ran down.
Hickory, dickory, dock!

Eenie, Meenie, Minie, Moe

Eenie, Meenie, Minie, Moe,
Catch a tiger by the toe.
If he hollers, let him go,
Eenie, Meenie, Minie, Moe.

If All The World

If all the world were apple pie,
And all the sea were ink,
And all the trees were bread and cheese,
What should we have for drink?